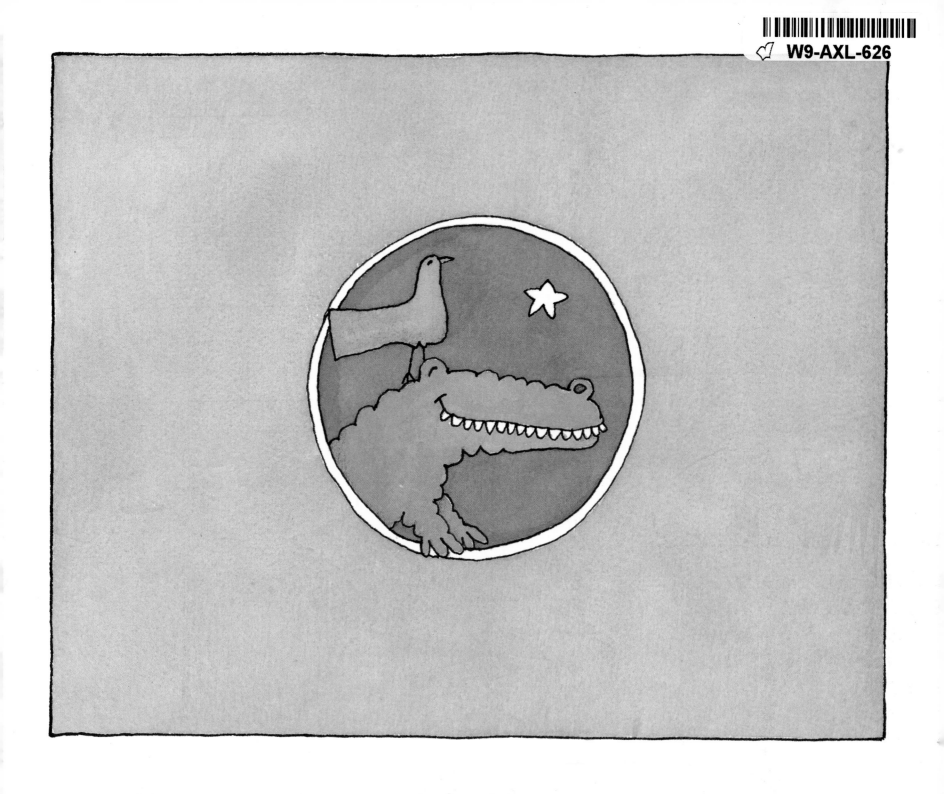

W9-AXL-626

Bill and Pete

Go Down the Nile

written and illustrated by **Tomie dePaola**

G. P. Putnam's Sons · New York

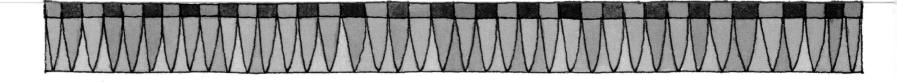

For David U. and Margaret F.
who like to travel

Text and illustrations copyright © 1987 by Tomie dePaola. All rights reserved. This book, or parts thereof, may not be reproduced in any form without permission in writing from the publisher. G.P. Putnam's Sons, a division of The Putnam & Grosset Group, 200 Madison Avenue, New York, NY 10016. Sandcastle Books and the Sandcastle logo are trademarks belonging to The Putnam & Grosset Group. First Sandcastle Books edition, 1990. Published simultaneously in Canada. Printed in Hong Kong by South China Printing Co. (1988) Ltd. Library of Congress Cataloging-in-Publication Data dePaola, Tomie. Bill and Pete go down the Nile. Summary: Little William Everett Crocodile and his friend Pete, a toothbrush, take a class trip to a Cairo museum where they encounter a jewel thief. [1. Egypt—Fiction. 2. Crocodiles—Fiction] 1. Title. PZ7.D439Bj 1987 [E] 86-12258

ISBN 0-399-21395-3 (hardcover)
5   7   9   10   8   6   4
ISBN 0-399-22003-8 (paperback)
1   3   5   7   9   10   8   6   4   2
First Sandcastle Books Impression

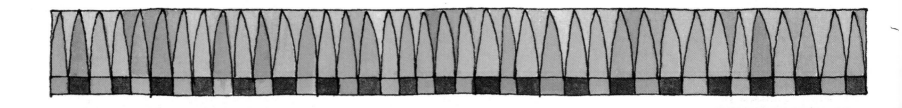

Tomorrow was the first day of school, and William Everett Crocodile
(who was called Bill) and his friend Pete (who was his toothbrush)
were getting ready.
"Don't forget your new pencil box, Bill," said Mama.
"And your new lunch box," said Pete.
"It will be so nice to see Ms. Ibis again, Mama," said Bill.
"I wonder what you'll learn this year?" said Mama.

The next morning, after kissing Mama goodbye,
Bill and Pete started out for school.

It was fun to see all the other little crocodiles again.

"Now class," said Ms. Ibis, "we are going to start this school year
by studying the history and geography of Egypt and the River Nile."
"Oh goody!" cried all the children.

"What did you learn today, Bill?" asked Mama.
"We learned all about the River Nile, Mama," said Bill.
"It's nice to learn about your own hometown," said Mama.

On Tuesday Ms. Ibis told the class about the sphinx.

"Today we learned about the stinks, Mama," said Bill.
"You mean *sphinx*, Bill," said Pete.
"And boy, is it weird looking!"

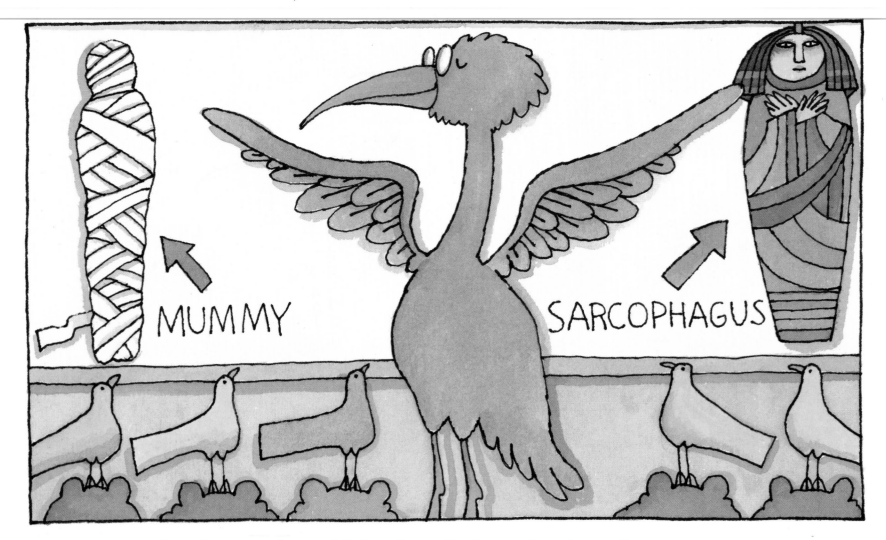

MUMMY

SARCOPHAGUS

On Wednesday Ms. Ibis told the class all about the Pharaohs,
the pyramids and mummies.
"The Pharaohs built the pyramids so they could be buried there
with all their riches," Ms. Ibis told them. "When they died,
they were wrapped up in long strips of cloth and called mummies.
The mummy was put in a beautiful case called a sarcophagus."

"What did you learn today, Bill?" said Mama.

"Oh, Mama, we learned about the Pharaohs and the pyramids," said Bill.

"We learned about mummies and esophaguses."

"You mean *sarcophaguses,*" said Pete.

"How exciting," said Mama.

On Thursday Ms. Ibis told the class about the Sacred Eye of Isis.
"It is the most valuable jewel in all the world," said Ms. Ibis.
"OOOOO," said all the little crocodiles.
"But," she added, "there is a saying that whoever owns it
  has bad luck."
"OOOOO," said all the little crocodiles.

"That is why it is kept in the Royal Museum," said Ms. Ibis.
"Now, how would you like to see the sphinx, the pyramids
  and the Sacred Eye of Isis?"
"Oh yes," said all the little crocodiles.
"Well, tomorrow we are going to take a class trip down the Nile."
"Hurray!" they all shouted.

"Do you have your lunch box?" asked Mama.

"Yes, Mama," said Bill.

"Now Pete, don't forget to brush Bill's teeth," said Mama.

"I won't," said Pete.

"Have a good time and listen to Ms. Ibis and do what she says," said Mama.

"Goodbye, Mama," said Bill and Pete.

"Does everyone have their partners?" Ms. Ibis asked.
"Yes, Ms. Ibis," the crocodiles answered.
"Then, forward, swim."

"OOOOO," said all the little crocodiles. "There's the Grand Hotel."

"OOOOO," said all the little crocodiles. "There's the sphinx."

"Bill," said Pete, "look at that man in the big car with all the ladies."
"He must be a Pharaoh," said Bill.
"Watch out for the Bad Guy," whispered an old crocodile
   to Bill and Pete as he swam by.

"Stay in line," said Ms. Ibis as the *Nile Queen* went by.
"OOOOO," said all the little crocodiles.

"Here we are at the pyramids," said Ms. Ibis as the class stepped ashore.
Ms. Ibis bought the tickets and they all went inside.

"The guide will hold a big mirror to help light up the passageway so
we can see," Ms. Ibis explained to the class. "Now, as I told you all,
the mummies and all the riches are no longer kept here. They are in
the Royal Museum, which we will visit next. And where we will see . . ."
"The Sacred Eye of Isis—OOOOO," said all the little crocodiles.

The class saw mummies, and sarcophaguses—
and the Sacred Eye of Isis.

"There's that man again, Bill," whispered Pete.
"He sure looks familiar."

And then they sat down to eat their lunch.
"Ms. Ibis, may I be excused, please," said Bill,
    and he and Pete went inside to find a rest room to brush Bill's teeth.

"Aha! Look, Bill," said Pete.

"I thought I recognized him. The *Bad Guy!*"

"Oh, Mr. Bad Guy. *Don't!*" cried Bill. "You'll have *bad luck!*"

"Shut up, you walking suitcase!" yelled the Bad Guy,
and he locked Bill inside a sarcophagus.

"You can't do that to my friend," shouted Pete,
and he flew into the rest room to get some toilet paper.

"Take that!" said Pete, and he flew around and around.
And presto — the Bad Guy was a *mummy!*

Then Pete untied a guard who let Bill out of the sarcophagus.

"Where have you been, William Everett!" scolded Ms. Ibis.
"Why, these two fine fellows saved the Sacred Eye of Isis
   from falling into evil hands," said the head of the museum.
"The Bad Guy is being taken to Cairo and put in jail.
   And as a reward, we're going to send you all home on the *Nile Queen*."

"OOOOO," said all the little crocodiles.

"And so, Mama, that's what happened on our first class trip," said Bill.

"My goodness," said Mama. "What an adventure."

"And Ms. Ibis was right," said Bill.

"The Sacred Eye of Isis *does* bring bad luck."

"Especially to Bad Guys," said Pete.